Jeffrey Grenfell-Hill

Jeffrey Grenfell-Hill trained for the professional theatre at the Bristol Old Vic Theatre School, where he was chosen to be the student director in the final year. After a lecture tour of American colleges, universities, and performing arts centres, he was invited to join the examining board of the London Academy of Music and Dramatic Art .

His poems have appeared in Penguin and Heinemann anthologies. Samuel French have published his plays, and his monologues have been published by Oberon Books in an anthology edited by Shaun McKenna. He is the author of two collections: *Monologues and Duologues for Young Actors* and *Monologues and Duologues for the Drama Studio*. His monologues and duologues have been chosen for the LAMDA examination syllabus for the Acting exams as "set pieces". They are often performed as "own choice" selections at major festivals of Speech and Drama.

Jeffrey himself is an adjudicator of many years' standing with a doctorate from the University of Wales. He was Director of Sixth-Form Studies at St. George's School, Harpenden, where he taught A/S and A level Theatre Studies. He continues as an Examiner for the London Academy of Music and Dramatic Art .

Jeffrey is a Knight Commander of the Order of St. John of Jerusalem.

First published in the UK in 2023 by Aurora Metro Publications Ltd
80 Hill Rise, Richmond, TW106UB
www.aurorametro.com   info@aurorametro.com
T: @aurorametro FB/AuroraMetroBooks
Blighty (1914-1918) © 2023 Jeffrey Grenfell-Hill
Cover photo: Wikimedia public domain. British troops occupying German dugouts in the Battle of the Somme 1916.
Cover designed by Aurora Metro Books.
With many thanks to: Audrey de Leon and Ines Almeida

ISBN: 978-1912430-74-1- print
978-1-912430-75-8 -ebook

BLIGHTY
(1914-1918)

by

Jeffrey Grenfell-Hill

AURORA METRO BOOKS

Private Arthur Grenfell, the author's great uncle, killed in 1916, aged 20. This play is dedicated to him.

CONTENTS

ABOUT THE PLAY

The inspiration and motivation to write this play came from a photograph I have of my grandfather's youngest brother, Arthur Grenfell, who was killed on March 31st 1916. He was just 20 years old and was part of that first tranche of conscripts called up by the government to serve in the trenches in late January 1916 when there was an urgent need to replace the great number of men who had been killed. They were doomed youth being marched off to war – Arthur only lasted 2 months.

As a social historian and a dramatist I believe that historic events can best be appreciated and remembered when presented in a narrative form. The history teacher ought to harness the power of drama to improve awareness of the emotional impact of key events on ordinary people, thus encouraging empathy.

When I was teaching Yr.9 World War 1 history I researched this period and used photographs, posters, poems, diaries, memoirs and letters to support what we were all learning about life in the trenches.

I wanted to highlight the role of the Voluntary Aid Detachment (VAD) as these women and girls were crucial to the care of wounded men in the military hospitals. This was all preparatory to our Yr.9 trip to the battlefields and cemeteries of Flanders. It further informed me and has inspired me to write *Blighty (1914-1918)*.

Thinking in terms of performance I wanted to write a play which would be easy to perform in either a classroom, a drama studio or a stage area. My intention was to create a text which was adaptable in both staging and casting. Chairs, benches, boxes or rostra can be utilised. The narrator can be gender changed, as can the Newsboy.

Where Musical Theatre is taught I wanted an opportunity to develop the vocal skills available instead of relying on recording the songs .

I hope this play will be inspirational. It is my intention to position *Blighty (1914-1918)* as a central link to key departments within a school so that pupils may have deeper cultural understanding. Moreover, there might be cross-curricula links with the History, English, Music, Art and Drama Departments adding their own specialisation values to a full understanding of what *Blighty (1914-1918)* is revealing.

I believe this is a powerful play, not only for schools, but for the wider theatre arena .

– Jeffrey Grenfell-Hill

Swansea Little Theatre, who have a tradition of supporting creative writing by Welsh authors, will showcase *Blighty (1914-1918)* at their Club Night meeting in the spring of 2023 in the Dylan Thomas Theatre.

This event has been arranged by Dreena Morgan-Harvey, Director of the Theatre, who will be supported by members of the Theatre Company in a staged play reading.

BLIGHTY (1914 – 1918)

Jeffrey Grenfell-Hill

A play in two acts

CHARACTERS

NARRATOR
VERA
LUCY
HEADMASTER
STAR
MAN 1
MAN 2
MAN 3
FRITZ
NEWSBOY
STAR
OLD MAN 1
OLD MAN 2
JOEY
TAFFY
GREG
EDWIN
WENTWORTH
CAPTAIN

OFFICER
OFFICER'S SERVANT
SERGEANT
SOLDIERS 1, 2, 3, 4
ALF
LEN
BEN
GERMAN
SID
EDMUND
OLLIE
GEORGE
RON
ERNIE
MRS. PARKER
MAMA
BERT
ENTERTAINER
JACK
VOICE

Note

The company can be made up of 9 actors. As this is meant to be an ensemble play in the style of a Brecht production, as many as 15 to 20 actors could be participants in the action.

An ethnic mix in the company would reflect the multi-ethnicity of the British Army during this war. Empire troops fought in the front-line trenches.

To support the diversity of the troops there should be different accents. Taffy, for example is South Walian; Ron is from Preston.

Costumes could be as simple or as complicated as the director thinks fit.

All the Vesta Tilley songs could be performed rather than just used as sound effects.

If the text is too long as a performance, some scenes can be omitted, and the playing time shortened.

ACT ONE

The acting area is made up of different rostra of varying sizes. It would help if these had wheels. The rostra can then be positioned to appropriately reflect the action. Different shapes can be created to suggest the various sections of a trench or location. Within the stage area is a large prop table. The actors can take whatever hat or accoutrement they might need to suit their role. Various props can be collected to further support the action and the mimed sequences. The actors remain on stage throughout and may be used as supportive troops if required to suggest there are other participants in the action.

NARRATOR *(Stands at the side of the rostra. Spotlight.)* It is the Summer of 1914, and we in England are more concerned with the problem of Home Rule in Ireland than tensions and assassinations in the Balkans. And who knows where they are on a map? *(laughs and shrugs his shoulders)* We are all far too concerned about the Irish problem. The Protestants of the north do not want to be a minority in a united Ireland...

Our newspaper headlines are dominated by the Irish question... that's what we are all talking about... and of course polite society is talking about the scandalous use of "not bloody likely" by Eliza Shaw's Pygmalion. First-nighters and critics were utterly shocked... there is also newspaper coverage of those hysterical suffragettes... they are always up to their criminal antics, concealing hammers in their muffs and jumping in front of horses...

Lights fade and rise again. A Newsboy appears with a placard and crosses the stage. This happens periodically.

NEWSBOY *(He waves a newspaper)* Read all about it! War declared on Germany. Read it for yourselves...

SCENE 1

The breakfast room in a middle-class home.

VERA *(Sitting at a table with a newspaper)* To think that up until now what dominated my mind was the suffragette movement and their very public demonstrations. Until this morning, my mind was set on a faraway fable of window smashing, suffragettes throwing bombs and damaging pictures in public galleries...

NEWSBOY Hundreds of Belgian babies viciously bayoneted by German troops.

VERA Just think... at the beginning of this week, my only worries were being bombarded as usual with infuriating requests to help with jumble sales, 'wait' at bazaar teas, play in amateur theatricals and to take the place of tiresome individuals who had fallen out at Bridge... Yes, indeed! I lived in the restless, critical, busy-busy atmosphere of a pre-war provincial town...doesn't that sound odd..."Pre-war?"

NEWSBOY *(He waves a newspaper.)* Thousands of Belgian women and children murdered in their beds! Read all about it

VERA *(Shaking her head in disbelief)* Upon reflection, I cannot believe that I entirely failed to notice in the daily papers of June 29th an account of the assassination of a European potentate whose name was unknown to me, in a Balkan town of which I had never heard. I don't think even Papa remarked on it at the breakfast table, and even Mama was probably encased in her usual self-satisfaction at how well she was organising her part of the church fete.

The lights fade on her and a spotlight appears on the Narrator.

NARRATOR How many millions had never heard of the Archduke Franz Ferdinand of Austria? How many millions could not point to Sarajevo on a map? *(He shakes his head.)* The assassin's bullet triggered a blood bath...

Spotlight fades to the newsboy.

NEWSBOY *(Shouting as he crosses the stage again.)* King and Country need you! King and Country need you! *(Waves newspaper)* Join up to fight the Hun!

The lights focus on Vera again.

VERA   My brother's speech day is etched in my mind as the last day of a vanished world...I remember the Headmaster said, in a slow decisive voice at the end of his address...

HEADMASTER *(In a spotlight standing as if at a podium)* And remember this, boys, as you approach manhood: that if a man cannot be useful to his country, he is better dead.

The light fades on him.

VERA   For a moment, there was a terrible and indescribable foreboding, then the boys went up to get their prizes.

NEWSBOY   *(Dramatising the headlines)* German bombardment of Flemish towns. Read all about thousands of deaths. *(Waving a newspaper)* The shelling of innocents in their homes.

VERA *(In astonishment)* There was immediate German hatred. One week we are listening to German bands in the park, buying pastries from German bakers on the High Street, and the next we are meant to hate them... I find it all utterly astonishing.

The lights fade on her and rise again.

SCENE 2

Two men approach a man on the street, who is very aware that he is being threatened.

MAN 1   Look who we've found: Fritz the fancy waiter from the fancy Palace Hotel.

MAN 2   Fritz, the bloody Hun.

FRITZ   No! I am not a German. I am Austrian from Vienna.

MAN 1   Who are you kidding? You're all the same. *(He grabs Fritz by the throat.)* You're just a lying German shit.

MAN 2 *(Delivering a blow to Fritz's stomach)* Take that for bayonetting babies.

MAN 1 *(Hitting him across the head)* And that's for murdering women.

FRITZ   Please no more! *(Trying to fend off the blows)* I am an innocent man.

MAN 2   Like bloody hell you are!

They beat Fritz up and then lift him and throw him over a rostrum.

MAN 1   Yeah! That's how we deal with bloody German bastards.

MAN 2   Bloody murderers.

The two men walk off with their arms around each other's shoulders.

Light fades on them and rises again.

VERA   The German waiter from The Palace Hotel has multiple injuries having been thrown over a wall, and the German baker on the High Street has had his windows smashed in. I find it incomprehensible that hatred could erupt so quickly, so easily, and in such an intense manner.

Light fades on Vera and rises again.

SCENE 3

All the actors move to the front of the stage and sit in a semi-circle with their backs to the audience. As the lights come up again, they focus their attention on stage centre where a Music Hall star appears. They stop talking to each other and applaud and cheer in an enthusiastic manner.

There is a musical introduction to "Your King and Country Want You".

STAR *(Singing in a vibrant and dramatic manner)* "We don't want to lose you..."

The Star focuses on the men in the audience as she sings the song.

Lights fade and rise again.

SCENE 4

We see a young upper-class woman.

LUCY   The atmosphere is all so thrilling. My family has a small estate here in Kent, and Papa has already got the footmen to sign up. He says it's wrong to keep male servants hanging around the manor when there are Germans to fight. I've gathered a bag full of white feathers, and I intend to take them to Canterbury and hand them out to any young man not in uniform... we have a glorious fight on our hands, and it could be over before we know it... *(She walks off.)*

The Star crosses the stage in an animated manner singing, "We don't want to lose you."

The lights fade and rise again.

SCENE 5

A street in Canterbury. Three young men appear sauntering along. They are accosted by Lucy.

LUCY *(Calling out in an animated manner)* Cowards! I can spot you... *(Goes up to them as she fumbles in her bag for the white feathers)* Three cowards! Why are you not at the recruiting centre signing up to fight for your country?

MAN 1   Miss, my Ma's a widow, she needs me at home.

MAN 2   My old man's unemployed, Miss.

MAN 3   My Ma needs the money I bring in.

MAN 1   If I don't bring in my wages, my Ma can't put food on the table.

LUCY   What rot! Just a load of excuses. Do you want to be cowards or heroes? If I were a man, I'd be off like a shot! I would be in uniform by now and ready to go... So, this is what you get from me, and I hope it makes you feel guilty *(She gives each one a white feather)*. The action will be over by Christmas, and you'll regret it all your lives... it's a shilling a day at the Front, and your Mas will not lack money.

The lights gradually fade, then focus on the song. The Star crosses the stage again, singing her song.

The lights fade and then come up again on Lucy.

SCENE 6

*Lucy is outside riding around her father's estate. She sits
sideways on a rostrum and then jumps down. She carries
a riding crop.*

LUCY   I feel this is my patriotic duty. To ride
around our estate and get the young farm
hands to join up. What use are our young
men when the estate can function quite
well with the older men doing the jobs?
Indeed, some of the old codgers who live on
Papa's generosity can jolly well pull their
socks up and pitch in to do some work, the
old men can take over from the young men.

*Two young men appear and mime digging and hoeing.
They are engaged in farm work.*

LUCY *(Going up to them)* You are the Harris boys, are you
not, from Home Farm? *(They stop digging
and deferentially take off their caps.)*

MAN 1   Yes, Miss Lucy. We have to clear this half-
acre by nightfall.

MAN 2   We've been at it since daybreak.

LUCY   You know that we are at war with Germany?

MAN 1   Yes, Miss Lucy.

MAN 2   We have been for a week, Miss Lucy.

LUCY   Then why are you not in uniform? I have a
whole bag of white feathers here, but I am
sure you will both do the right thing and
join up before it's all over.

MAN 1   Our Pa says we should go.

MAN 2   But our Ma is dead against it. When we
bring it up, she starts crying and saying it's
the politicians' fight, not ours.

MAN 1   Sobbing sometimes...

MAN 2   We only be sixteen and seventeen, Miss Lucy.

LUCY   That's old enough. Indeed, you both look older. I'm sure that once you are both in uniform that your Ma will be proud of you...

MAN 1   Our Ma says we are too short for the army anyways...

LUCY   Nonsense! Five foot three is tall enough to serve. And both of you must be five foot six at least, so that's big enough! So off you go, be brave!

The two young farm labourers put their agricultural implements to rest on their shoulders and march off like soldiers. Lucy gets back up on to the side of a rostra as if ridding side-saddle.

Lights fade, then come up again.

SCENE 7

Two old men are seated smoking pipes.

OLD MAN 1 *(Shaking his head)* This is one big fuss I can tell you... bigger, a lot bigger than the Boer War.

OLD MAN 2 *(Nodding)* Aye! I reckon afore long you and me will have to go back to work and shift our backsides and pitch in! We old 'uns will be needed on the Home Front.

OLD MAN 1 That's it! If the young 'uns go, it will be up to us.

OLD MAN 2 Aye! But I ain't doing nothin' for nothin' to be patriotic. I want a shilling for work done.

OLD MAN 1 You mean old bugger. *(Laughing at him)*

OLD MAN 2 *(Lifting his hands)* These seventy-year-old hands can still do the work. And work needs to be paid for... I can be patriotic enough when I'm making a shilling or two in the war work.

He ends up chuckling.

The light fades on the men and comes up on the Narrator.

NARRATOR Men are clamouring to be soldiers here and all over Europe. It is as if the brake has been released on some huge martial juggernaut. Now it has begun to roll so decisively, there is nothing in the world that will stop it.

Armaments will blow us all to bits, to smithereens... the lamps are going out all over Europe and the furnace of hate is being systematically stoked... it will become a raging inferno...God help us all.

The light fades as we hear... "Keep the Home Fires Burning".

From now on, the action is all at the front. The rostra are used to denote the trenches, dugouts, and relief stations.

Throughout the rest of the performance, there are various degrees of war sounds, machine guns, bombardment. A barrage of noises. The intensity of which will vary according to the action. It is constant and unforgiving.

But sometimes muted, depending on the action. It must be unceasing.

Lights come up.

SCENE 8

A firing trench with men in various positions .

JOEY *(Crouching down further)* God Almighty! They've got it in for us today... Let's crouch down deeper mate.

GREG This trench is one hell of a muddy maze *(He crouches down deeper)* And it's full of bloody rats.

JOEY I bet there are ten rats to every man.

GREG Probably more... and as big as cats *(He mimes kicking one away.)* Get off me! Ugh! I hate them. They get big on eating dead horses.

JOEY And dead men.

GREG You're giving me the horrors.

JOEY Out there in No Man's Land is rat heaven.

GREG Mind, the German shells can blow them to smithereens too.

JOEY Yeah! Human life and rat life is cheap out here.

A long pause as they listen to the barrage.

GREG Can you hear that bombardment getting stronger?

The bombardment gets louder.

JOEY   God forbid! They're softening us up for another Putsch.

One of the other men comes forward and talks directly to the audience. He stands in a pool of light.

EDWIN   Back home they talk about our trenches as just one long drawn-out hiding place. Back in 'Blighty' they can't visualise the complexity of it all. Here at the front, it's a complicated system well thought out. *(He laughs)* Although hellishly muddy in places. Each infantry trench has two others behind it: a support trench and then a reserve trench behind that. This network is connected by a communications trench, along this one comes our supplies and the relief infantry. The engineers lay down the telegraph cables along the reserve trench. We, the infantry... the foot soldiers... we call ourselves the P.B.I., yeah! The P.B.I. and do you know what that stands for? The Poor Bloody Infantry, because we do the hardest fighting stuck in the firing trench.

There is a flash of bright lights and a terrific explosion. Edwin reacts by dropping to his knees.

EDWIN   This firing trench is dug out in clever 'zig-zag' sections to minimise damage. Only a small area would be affected if attacked by the Huns or hit by a shell.

Another heavy barrage and Edwin crouches. The newsboy appears and crosses the stage.

NEWSBOY   Flanders. Fighting rages around Ypres. Many casualties...Germans must be stopped... Read all about it.

EDWIN *(Getting up off the floor and going stage centre)* Any minute now Lieutenant Wentworth will blow his whistle and the sergeant will shout: "Get up and go over the top!" and out we will all have to go with our bayonets at the ready. All for a shilling a day... it's the hot shrapnel I hate, it hits my helmet like hot cinders from a raging inferno... wish me luck... I need it. I could be blown to smithereens and never get back to 'Blighty' to see my Ma.

Edwin returns to the other men as a barrage kicks in, and they mime getting ready to go over the top.

The light fades and rises again.

SCENE 9

We see an officer's dugout where Lieutenant Wentworth and another junior officer are censoring their men's letters. They sit at a table.

WENTWORTH *(Reading a letter)* I suppose this censoring business is a way of getting to know the men a little better.

OFFICER Yes! If only the letters were more interesting, I could nod off and go to sleep sometimes.

WENTWORTH *(Laughing)* Surely, they are all too short for that!

OFFICER Yes. Some of them seem to have more kisses than text.

WENTWORTH   I read one yesterday with eighteen kisses: three lines of six after a very short message to his mother.

OFFICER   Have you noticed how the men seem to write regularly to their mothers, but hardly ever to their fathers?

WENTWORTH I think it's because they want to reassure their mothers that all is well.

OFFICER   Indeed! Listen to this: "Dear Ma, everything is fine here, and my pals keep me in good spirits. Remember me to Polly and her family." Then twelve kisses.

WENTWORTH   We have to remember they are mostly elementary school boys; they left school at twelve or thirteen. They haven't the skills that we have, the vocabulary.

OFFICER   Of course, but every now and again, one reads a letter which places a man in a distinctly good class.

WENTWORTH   Probably a Grammar school boy.

OFFICER   Yes! But what a lesson it is to read the thoughts of a man, refined, and sensitive as we are without the advantages of birth and education.

WENTWORTH   When you get one like that, do share it with me. I find the common soldier writes in a very commonplace manner.

OFFICER   Wentworth, old chap, you have to admit they send more kisses than we do.

WENTWORTH It's to fill up the space.

The light fades, and then there is a spotlight.

NARRATOR The Germans have taken the higher ground, which gives them a tactical advantage. But when I say higher, I mean only a matter of a metre or two above sea level. Our British trenches are nightmarish, and our men live in the foulest conditions. There is a never-ending struggle against water and mud. Wrapped in their groundsheets, the men snatch a few hours' sleep – the sleep of the exhausted. No one now believes that the war will be over by Christmas; that prospect has vanished. This is a world of mud, barbed wire, and craters.

Lights fade and come up again.

SCENE 10

Another part of a trench where the men are huddled in their ground sheets in various positions. Some stand on the fire step using primitive periscopes to observe the Germans from below the firing line. A barrage lights the sky.

A sergeant appears with a big jar of rum.

SERGEANT Right, lads! Line up for your rum ration. Get into some sort of queue.

The men line up with their tin cans and the sergeant starts to dole out the rum.

SERGEANT *(Enthusiastically)* This will warm the cockles of your heart...yes! The cockles of your heart.

SOLDIER 1 Who is he kidding?

SOLDIER 2 We all know it. It's to give us Dutch courage.

SOLDIER 3 I could do with a dose of courage.

SOLDIER 1 No sooner do we get it, than it's "get up and over boys!"

SOLDIER 4 Horrible stuff, I hate it.

SOLDIER 3 Yeah! But you drink it, Alf! Don't you? Down the hatch it goes.

SOLDIER 2 I wonder how much the Sarge gives himself? He's in charge of the bottle.

SOLDIER 1 A treble allowance more likely. He's got a lot of cockles to warm!

Some of the men laugh. They take up various positions in the trench to drink their rum and smoke a cigarette.

Lights fade then come up again. There is a disturbance as some rats appear in the trench.

SCENE 11

The men react to the arrival of the rats in the trench.

ALF *(Spotting a rat)* God forbid! Look at the size of that one... that one there, it's the size of a cat.

BEN You're jittery. I thought a country boy like you would be used to rats.

ALF Not rats like cats; we had a ratting terrier that was a champion at getting them!

BEN That's why the Captain has his terrier with him. Officer's privilege and a champion ratter he is.

ALF   Come on, let's get spades and smash 'em to a pulp. Where there's five, there will be fifty!

The men get spades and mime hitting and killing the rats.

The rat attack is interrupted by Lieutenant Wentworth blowing his whistle repeatedly and shouting orders.

WENTWORTH *(Shouting)* Get up and go! Over the top, lads, each and every one of you. Steady yourselves and once over, keep on firing... keep it up... give the Huns all you've got.

Heavy artillery is heard in the background as the men scramble up and over the rostra. We hear steady firing, the men shouting, and lights flashing from flares. A heightened barrage continues with a commotion all along the trenches. Other officers are blowing their whistles. There is machine gunfire. A barrage continues.

The lights gradually dim and then come up again.

As the exhausted men scramble back into the trench and take up various positions, they light up cigarettes and settle down. The background noise diminishes.

Lights fade and rise again.

SCENE 12

Another part of a front-line trench. Men sit or stand in different positions.

Lights up on two soldiers.

TAFFY *(Shivering and rubbing his hands together)* This cold is getting into my bones... freezing them... I could do with a nice cuppa tea.

RON   There's nothing nice about the tea we get here! They put too much chloride of lime in it to kill the germs... water like that ain't going to make nice tea!

TAFFY   You're always complaining... can't you be cheerful for once?

RON   What's cheerful about this? There's a lot to complain about. If I had a choice, I'd have another rum ration and put it in my tea. Rum would cheer me up no end even if it's half a gill...

TAFFY   If they put lots of sugar in it, you don't taste the lime so much. Tea warms you up... it's a nice comforter.

RON   Rum would warm you up quicker, mate...

TAFFY   Let's face up to it, the Huns chuck everything they can at us and we'll just have to grin and bear it.

RON   And drink our bloody tea...

There is silence.

TAFFY   Hang on, Ron... it's silent... there's no bloody barrage... Hey! Can you hear it? The Huns are singing.

From the German lines, the sound of 'Heilage Nacht' being sung.

RON   Lord in Heaven! The Huns have stopped shelling us... Do you know what it is? It's Christmas Eve...

They listen to the Germans singing.

RON   Hey! We can do better than that...

TAFFY *(Turning to the other soldiers)* Come on boys! Let's give them our words... we all know the tune and can sing out loud.

The men in the trench all sing 'Silent Night'. After they have finished, a German voice is heard, calling out across the lines.

GERMAN   Tommy! Can you hear me?

BEN   Yeah! We can hear you loud and clear...

GERMAN   We wish you a Happy Christmas... Ein Fröhliche Weihnachten.

Silence.

BEN   We don't know any German, but we can be friendly too. Come on, boys, let's wish Jerry a "Happy Christmas."

The men call out their greetings across the trenches, English and German combining; they sing 'Silent Night' in unison using their own language.

Lights dim, then they pick out three men.

TAFFY   I'd love one of my Ma's mince pies and a glass of ginger wine.

ALF   Ginger wine! Was your Ma a teetotaller?

TAFFY   Yeah! Welsh Baptist. She's taken the pledge. Alcohol never touches her lips.

BEN   I'd like a slice of Christmas cake.

ALF   I'd like a double rum ration just to wish us all a Happy Christmas.

TAFFY   You mean to have a Merry Christmas then...

ALF   Yeah! Cos I haven't taken the pledge.

BEN   I get the shivers when the Sarge appears with that rum jar: it means "up and over" and each time I think it's over for me... my number's up and I'll never get back to 'Blighty'.

Lights fade on the three men and then come up again.

SCENE 13

The same trench.

BEN *(Shaking his head and talking directly to the audience)* Lies, all lies! The war wasn't over by Christmas... there was on-going hell for all of us. Each one of us cowering in our own private misery, hoping there will be a day when the rum won't appear... a day when we don't go up the scaling ladders and march into hell...

There is a flash of light as a barrage intensifies.

BEN   Yes! I get the shivers, alright, when Lieutenant Wentworth appears with the Sergeant and the rum ration... the whistle... the Sergeant shouting "Up and over boys!", and we all go scrambling out of the trench into no-man's land. They should call it 'Dead Man's land,' that's the truth of it. The mates you had and didn't get back are all out there rotting away. And I don't mean neat dead bodies all intact. I mean bits of bodies... shells that blew their heads off... split their skulls apart...

Sometimes you have to run over them. It's hell, the shells, the German machine guns mowing us down... the Huns throwing all they can at us... the ground shaking under your feet...

I can't take this anymore. However many fags I smoke, my nerves are shattered. But I got a plan: in five days' time, I'm due for leave to 'Blighty'. I'll be home, and my Ma's gone as cook to Bromley Manor, so she can hide me in one of the gardeners' sheds on the estate. All the gardeners have enlisted... the gardens are overgrown, so I'll hide meself, desert, and not come back... they shoot you here for desertion but not at home in 'Blighty'. You get sent to prison. But they have to find you first, and no-one knows where my Ma has gone to work. Sometimes it pays to be called Mrs Jones...

There is a loud blast and shrapnel falls into the trench. Ben falls down, indicating his fear, and remains on the ground.

BEN *(Still cowering)* Lord Bromley's gone and given the manor over to the army as a convalescent home for wounded soldiers, so no-one's going to notice me arriving and disappearing. Ma says the gardens are going to wrack and ruin, as no-one cares... it's a shambles. I could hide and be safe there until this bloody war is over. Our trench fills with water, it is damn freezing, and I don't want to get trench foot and have my legs amputated...

Lights fade, then come up again.

SCENE 14

Two officers are seated at a table in their dug out, looking at a line-up of jars which have just arrived.

WENTWORTH *(Tapping one of the jars with his officer's stick)* This new delivery of jars doubles our rum ration for the men, Sir!

CAPTAIN We weren't ready for yet more rum, Wentworth. It's a mystery to me. We'll have to stack them up with the others.

WENTWORTH Mysteries are rather worrying. Are they not, Sir?

CAPTAIN These jars look brand new. *(Picking one up)* Not at all like re-fills... jars that get knocked about a bit.

WENTWORTH The men love their rum ration, Sir. There'd be trouble if we ran out of the stuff... better to have a top up.

CAPTAIN *(Uncorking a jar)* I've never fancied rum myself *(He sniffs at the contents and grimaces.)* Good God! This stuff smells disgusting. *(Shaking his head.)* It's worse than the smell of gangrene, and that's bad enough. *(He offers Wentworth the jar to smell.)* Take a sniff of that Wentworth...

WENTWORTH Rather not, Sir, if you don't mind... take your word for it, absolutely... you're always right, Sir!

CAPTAIN What on earth are they expecting us to do with this ghastly stuff? *(Irritated)* And what on earth is it?

WENTWORTH Can't say, Sir. Shall we open this envelope that came with the jars?

CAPTAIN Good idea... throw some light on this delivery!

WENTWORTH *(Opening envelope and quickly scanning its contents)* It seems, Sir, that the jars are full of whale oil!

CAPTAIN Whale oil? Fighting a war with rum rations I can understand... but I thought whale oil was used in the manufacture of soap!

WENTWORTH *(Sifting through the papers)* It might be useful to see what our orders are, throw some light on this delivery. *(He finds a useful page and reads it.)* Wait 'til you read these orders, Sir!

CAPTAIN   You read them to me, Wentworth. I don't know where my glasses are at present.

WENTWORTH Right, Sir!

CAPTAIN   I can't wait to hear what we have to do with this disgusting stuff... not make soap for the troops, I hope!

WENTWORTH You won't believe the orders, Sir...

CAPTAIN   I will believe anything that comes from headquarters...

WENTWORTH Then what do you think of these orders then, Sir? *(He reads carefully)* "Because of the intense cold prevalent at this time, the following is advised for all men: before going out on patrol in these dire weather conditions, each man must be stripped of his clothes and rubbed with whale oil by an officer. This procedure will help to keep a man warm and prevent his body being frozen. An officer must see that it is done thoroughly."

CAPTAIN *(Shocked)* God forbid, Wentworth! What will headquarters think of next?

WENTWORTH God only knows, Sir, but what man would stand there naked and have an officer rub him down like a horse...

CAPTAIN   The men would refuse. It's a damn insult.

WENTWORTH The men would feel humiliated.

CAPTAIN   Yes! Greasing them up like a cooking pan, we would have a mutiny on our hands...

WENTWORTH Well, you could include me, Sir! As I am not rubbing whale oil on any of my men...

CAPTAIN   But we would be disobeying orders. *(Thinking about the problem)* Got it! We could say it never seemed cold enough for the men to freeze.

WENTWORTH I think I have a better solution, Sir. We have to get rid of this horrible stuff so... why don't we tell our men that the whale oil is to prevent trench foot and amputations. The men fear losing their feet to gangrene so we could order them to rub the oil into their own feet and up their legs... that way they do it themselves.

CAPTAIN *(Overjoyed)* Cracking idea, Wentworth! Good man! The men can do all their own rubbing... it will give them something to do, occupy their time... (*He laughs uproariously.*) We can empty the jars in no time at all and get rid of the ghastly stuff.

WENTWORTH Let's hope when we send these jars back empty to headquarters, they don't get mistakenly used for the rum ration...

CAPTAIN *(Pouring himself a drink)* That's why I'm sticking to cognac. Will you join me, Wentworth? *(He pours another drink and hands it over.)* Here's to 'problem solving' *(He raises his glass)*. Two heads are better than one, eh?

WENTWORTH Absolutely right, Sir!

Lights fade and then come up again.

SCENE 15

We see a group of soldiers in the reserve trench. The bombardment is heard at a distance, as the men are relaxing. They have their boots off and are applying the whale oil.

LEN   When the Sarge appeared with these jars, I thought we was getting a rum ration.

EDWIN   Not in the reserve trench, mate!

LEN   This stuff smells God awful. *(He applies the oil.)*

EDWIN   I'd put anything on my feet to prevent frostbite.

LEN   How much do you think we have to put on?

EDWIN   How the hell would I know? The Sarge said, "Plaster it on you lot and get on with it snappy quick..."

LEN   The frostbite amputees get sent home to 'Blighty'.

EDWIN   So, you think they're lucky going home with no feet? On bloody crutches for the rest of their lives!

There is silence as they work the whale oil into their feet and ankles.

LEN   I hope this stuff washes off easily before we go on home leave.

EDWIN   Do you think Lieutenant Wentworth is putting whale oil on his feet?

LEN   Not on your nellie, mate! He's probably been issued with crème-de-la- crème-de-bloody lavender...

EDWIN   I like the sound of that stuff!

Len laughs and rubs more oil.

The light dims as they begin to put their boots back on. In the background, a barrage increases in sound. Machine gun fire increases, then fades.

As the light dims, we hear Vesta Tilley singing "Tommy the Trench".

The lights are dim through the song, then come up on the narrator.

SCENE 16

NARRATOR The men try to sing when they can but there isn't a lot to sing about. If the rats don't plague them, it's the lice living in their shirts, their underclothes, in every garment. They run candles along the seams to kill them, but some scorch their clothes in the process. If it's possible to go to a divisional bathhouse, there are huge vats of hot water able to take ten or twelve men at a time. They splash around for ten or twelve minutes as their tunics and trousers are in the de-lousing machine... *(Shaking his head)* But so many eggs survive that a man's body heat gets them hatched, and it is scratch, scratch, scratch all over again. The Scots really suffer as their pleated kilts offer luxury accommodation to thousands of lice, then trench fever sets in...

Lights dim, and then they come up on the newsboy.

NEWSBOY *(Waving a newspaper. Carrying a placard)* Read all about it... We break through the

German front line. The Battle of Neuve Chapelle rages... we capture the high ground.

Light fades out, then light comes up again on the narrator.

NARRATOR *(Shaking his head)* Don't put up the bunting, don't wave any flags... the German Sixth Army has carried out a counterattack and halted our advance, but we are going to get Sappers to dig under the German positions and blow them to smithereens. They won't know what's hit them... the Spring of 1915 is going to be interesting.

Lights fade gradually as we hear a song: Vesta Tilley's song: "The Army of Today's All Right".

Black out.

Gradually, the lights come up.

SCENE 17

The scene is now a Red Cross Centre where a Voluntary Aid Detachment nurse is sitting at a table rolling up bandages. In the background, we hear the pounding of guns.

LUCY *(Carefully rolling up the bandages and putting them in a basket)* I've been here eighteen months. Day after day of amputees, of mutilated bodies... *(She wipes away tears.)* My parents were against my joining the VADs and coming over to France, but I had to assuage my feelings of guilt. You can't imagine the depth of self-hatred *(She wipes away more tears)* to think that I was rash enough to hand out white feathers in Canterbury. That I rode around my father's estate and urged our young men to fight for 'King and Country!' I made them feel like cowards... I called them cowards. *(Starts to cry again)* I had it in my stupid head that it would all be glorious, simply glorious and over by Christmas! Oh! How my words and actions haunt me now. Do you hear the guns? It never, ever stops....pounding... thudding....on and on, and each time they bring in a whole load of wounded, the guilt returns to me. Young men, seventeen, eighteen, my age, with their young bodies shattered, mutilated, their frightened eyes meeting mine. The guilt surges up in me whilst I sit beside a bed, holding the hand of a young man who is dying, and I have to be composed... nurse-like, but he's frightened and wants his Ma, and all I can do is squeeze his hand and pretend that he will pull through! But all I want to do is cry with him, for him and for myself... The guilt is always there... the terrible guilt!

Vera enters. She is also a VAD.

VERA   Matron has sent me looking for you.

LUCY   I thought she knew I was dealing with these bandages and having a cup of tea.

VERA   We are both to go to the German ward. A new batch of prisoners have just been brought in.

LUCY   There are no more beds available, they're all taken, Vera.

VERA   Then we will have to make them comfortable on the floor as best we can.

LUCY   Why is it always us?

VERA   Because we speak German. It's a comfort for them, especially the really bad cases.

LUCY *(Getting up)* I always open the windows when they die, to let their souls go out. *(Handing the basket of bandages to Vera).* Do you think I'm foolish?

VERA   No! But I'm glad there is loads to do and no time to think and grieve for them.

LUCY   Yes! Here we are nursing the prisoners and getting just as upset when they die in horrible pain as we do when our chaps die. They don't seem like the enemy, not when I'm holding the hand of a young Bavarian man who is dying of sepsis and wanting his mother to nurse him.

VERA   This is a topsy-turvy world. Yesterday, after I had re-bandaged the arm of a young German officer, he struggled to his feet, clicked his spurred heels together and bowed as he said 'thank you'. We could have been in a drawing room in Berlin.

LUCY   I have forgotten what a drawing room is like...

VERA   Come on, let's get a move on... duty calls.

LUCY   Duty, yes! But do you know what I think when I'm holding a dying man's hand?

VERA   What?

LUCY	An English hand, a German hand, they're all the same. They're mostly young men, seventeen, eighteen, our age... and they're dying and need comforting... loving one and hating the other isn't in my nature. *Ich kann sie nicht hassen, weil sie sterben.* [1]
VERA	I know, I think the same.

The lights fade and come up again.

SCENE 18

There is a lull in the fighting, and an accordion is heard being played from the German trenches. In the British trench, the men are resting and listening to the accordion.

SID	There he goes again, that Bavarian accordion player. He's good, very good.
RON	How close do you think he is?
SID	Maybe sixty yards away.
RON	And how do you know he's Bavarian? They're all Huns to me!
SID	Last time we went over, the uniforms had changed. Germany is made up of different states. A Bavarian isn't the same as a Prussian... a Prussian is nastier.
RON	How do you know so much? They didn't teach us all that at my school. It was all Germany and the Kaiser, and they're all Huns.

---

1   I cannot hate them as they die.

SID	I was footman to Lord Litchfield. You pick up a lot when you're waiting at table. Our so called 'betters' are big talkers especially the men when the ladies go off to have their coffee and the men get their port going round the table.
RON	So that's why you got nice hands then! Cos you handed the upper classes their port... posh bastards!
SID	These! *(He holds up his hands.)* They're not so nice now *(he laughs)* Lord Litchfield wouldn't have me waiting at table with hands like these! But we all wore white gloves in the dining room so he wouldn't see the dirt under my fingernails, would he? *(He laughs ironically.)* This is a different world...
OLLIE	I was a footman to Lord Bromley, and he sent us all out of the dining room when it was time for the port. They could speak freely then, and it got right noisy telling their tales... they passed the port round themselves, they didn't want us hearing what they said.
SID	There's differences in each household.
RON	Talking of toffs, look who's coming down our trench...
OLLIE	Lieutenant Wentworth, he's not too bad. He doesn't talk down to us like we're scum.
RON	A toff is a toff. I bet he's got his nice expensive body armour on. Money buys safety, our khaki is a death dress.

SID   Oh, cheer up! Lieutenant Wentworth doesn't speak to us like a bunch of school boys...

OLLIE   And he's gone down the side trench...

SID   Come on, let's have a song. Get your mouth organ out, Ollie. *(He starts to play.)*

All the men join in a song to the tune of 'What a friend we have in Jesus'.

MEN   When this lousy war is over.

                Oh, how happy we will be,

                When I get my civvy clothes on,

                No more soldiering for me.

                No more church parades on Sunday,

                No more putting in for leave.

                I will kiss the sergeant major,

                How I'll miss him, how I'll grieve.

As the song is being sung to a muted backdrop of gunfire, the lights fade.

ACT TWO

At this point, the stage area could be littered with helmets, spades and blankets. The image is one of debris. The sound of war picks up again: machine guns, artillery noises, flares, and shelling. Men have 'gone over', and we see them scrambling over the rostra back into the trench. All are in various stages of distress and fatigue. We hear cannonades and rockets.

The light gradually intensifies.

SCENE 1

A front line trench.

JACK *(Scrambling back into the trench and crying)*
Billy's gone... we've left him out there,
Edmund! I can't take it anymore... that's
done me in. It's a sight I won't forget, not
ever. *(He breaks down sobbing.)* Those
staring eyes... Billy's terrified eyes...

EDMUND *(Trying to comfort him)* There's nothing can
be done when a chap falls into a crater.

JACK I know that! The whole land out there is
full of bloody craters. One minute we were
all on the boards running back and then
Billy trips up, slides over and falls into that
crater and there's nothing, nothing we can
do! He's sinking into the mud, it isn't quick
like falling into a river, it's slow as the mud
pulled him down... down... *(He continues
to cry.)*

EDMUND You can't help else we'd drown in the mud
too... there's nothing you could have done.
*(He lights up a cigarette and offers it to
Jack.)* Here, have a smoke, calm you down.

JACK *(Pushing the cigarette away)* I don't want your
bloody fag!

EDMUND Okay, mate.

JACK Me and Billy go back a long way. We were
in village school together... we signed up
together. When Squire Stanton's daughter,
Miss Lucy, showed up and said we ought to
fight for our King...

EDMUND   And country! *(He continues to smoke.)* Yesterday Lieutenant Wentworth had to shoot a panic-stricken horse that fell into a crater...

JACK *(Agitated)* Yes! They can shoot a horse that's terrified and can't get back out, but not Billy *(He starts to cry again.)* Not Billy... he had to choke to death in the mud, smothered by it, and it was terrible to see him sinking deeper and deeper...

EDMUND   It's humane if you shoot a horse, but murder if it's a soldier.

JACK   This whole bloody war is murder. The Huns murder us, we murder them... and the mud in the craters is murderous. *(He starts to sob.)* What am I going to tell Billy's Ma when I get leave to Blighty again?

EDMUND   He will be classed as missing. I'd stick to that, Jack. You don't need to give his Ma the horrors... missing is kinder.

JACK   I just stood there and saw him choking to death.

EDMUND   You should have carried on running.

JACK   How can you leave your best mate even if you can't help him get out... I'd slip in too... slide in, there's nothing to send to his Ma. Nothing, Edmund... nothing at all!

EDMUND   But there wouldn't be if he's classed as missing...

JACK   I was a coward. Billy's gone... he was my best friend, and this damn war is never ending... it goes on and on...

There is a loud thunderclap as if a shell has hit the trench. Confusion. Strobe. Lighting. Highlights. The men being blown up and falling to the ground. This could be done in slow motion but should show in the end a trench with most men dead or wounded. Jack survives this attack, but he wanders around disorientated.

Lights dim, then rise on the narrator.

NARRATOR This war rages on... we fight our battles, gain a few yards, a village perhaps, but it's stalemate and the German spirit seems undimmed. They have grave casualties just as we do, there are grieving mothers when the death message comes, but the Huns are hoping a new weapon might shift the balance in their favour...after three years of fighting on two fronts they need a decisive breakthrough.

SCENE 2

A corner of a front-line trench.

SOLDIER *(Speaking directly to the audience)* When the first mustard gas came over, we were utterly unprepared. It's odourless and takes it's time creeping along – lethal. To say it terrified us, is an understatement. It is inhuman, barbarous, even worse than being machine gunned down or burned to a cinder by one of their flame-throwers. The Scots further up our trench were in bad shape... we call them kilties. They're proud of their kilts but in a gas attack it's terrible for them, the mustard gas burns their legs and their bums something terrible. Imagine the horror of it all... but now we've been issued with these *(holds up a gas mask),* but it's too late for some of the kilties who are now blind. This morning I was on stand-to... there I was with my gas mask on, listening to myself breathing... it is a strange sensation: your head is encased, and you try to breathe and peer out through the eyeglasses... I want to take it off, I want to be able to breathe unhindered. We inhabit a strange world of fellow zombies, but it's better to be a zombie than totally unprotected. The horses too have gas masks and play up and snort when they see them coming...

The soldier puts on his mask, and behind him, we see others doing the same.

The lights fade to twilight mode.

There is a disembodied upper class voice heard issuing instructions:

VOICE   If you are unfortunately caught in a gas attack without a gas helmet, the army issues these instructions which all men will strictly follow:

1. Take out your handkerchief.

2. Urinate into the material until it is soaked completely and utterly.

3. Tie it around your mouth and nose very tightly and breathe through it.

This procedure, if followed correctly, will help you get through the mustard attack.

Lights go to blackout, then rise on Vera.

SCENE 3

A Red Cross centre behind the firing line where VADS attend the wounded soldiers.

VERA *(Speaking directly to the audience)* We have ambulance trains jolting into the siding all day, all night, unloading gassed men shrieking and writhing... It is all so grotesque! My heart bleeds for the poor wretches. We were quite unprepared for this lethal new tactic, weapon, poisonous chemical...

Lucy, also wearing a VAD uniform, joins Vera.

LUCY So here you are, Vera, I've been looking for you.

VERA I had to come away for a moment. The men are in such excruciating pain...

LUCY I know, it is heart-breaking. I sometimes think I cannot go on, but these men need me, need us...

VERA I wish all those people back home who talk about going on with this war whatever the costs could see these soldiers suffering from mustard gas poisoning. Their great mustard-coloured blisters, blind eyes all sticky and stuck together, always fighting for breath...

LUCY   Yes! Gasping with their voices, when they find one, a mere whisper, saying their throats are closing and they know they will choke...

VERA *(Taking Lucy's hands)* We see it, Lucy, the blisters on their skin, the constant vomiting...

LUCY   And we know they have internal bleeding... it's horrible!

The two women hug each other for a moment.

VERA   It's far worse than the mutilations we attend to...

LUCY   And the amputees we nurse.

VERA   Come, duty calls... be brave like our men.

LUCY   I don't know for how much longer I can be brave...

They leave holding hands.

Light fades on them and comes up on the Narrator.

SCENE 4

NARRATOR The ambulance trains never cease to spill out their wounded, so many already half-dead. After a mustard gas attack, the men suffer the torments of hell! Blisters are found in any tender spot, most are the size of the palm of your hand...we are not talking about the little blisters you might get taking a hot pan out of an oven... these blisters are big, and they can be found in any tender and warm place, under the arms, between the legs, and over the face and neck. This is the horror of it all, and with sightless eyes the men shuffle along.

Lights fade and come up again on a row of men.

In a line with eyes bandaged, a group of soldiers, arms on each other's shoulders and led by Vera, shuffle ungainly across the stage. Lights fade then rise on the newsboy.

NEWSBOY *(Waving a paper)* Germany wages war with nerve gas! Read all about this terrible new weapon. Chemical warfare started on the Western Front... the Huns deploy new tactics...

Lights fade and rise on the Narrator.

NARRATOR Through the horror of it all, we are war-weary. Three years of deaths and casualties with no end in sight. At times it seems that God has forsaken us...but we are forbidden to think that!

Lights fade and rise on Wentworth.

SCENE 5

The officers' dug-out with table and chairs.

WENTWORTH *(Standing alone)* It's the shooting of the horses that tears at my heartstrings. I have always loved horses, and this is a war of horses and men... we could not function without horses, but sometimes they slide, lose their footing, and sink into the mud-filled craters... it's a slippery hell and we cannot get them out. I see the fear in their eyes as they snort and struggle, but there's nothing we can do. Only an officer can shoot them, and so my men come for me, and I have to get out my revolver and shoot the terrified animal... and it's all *(struggles with his emotions)* it's all so bloody awful, and I want to cry, but I can't, in front of the men. It has to be 'business like'; the regulation revolver shot and another horse dead, and I cannot even compose myself by breathing-in fresh air *(shakes his head despondently)*.There's no such thing as fresh air, it's all polluted with smoke, gun smoke, barrage smoke, cordite, the stink from the latrines, rat urine, our urine...I sometimes think that I shall never ever breathe in anything sweet ever again. Oh! How I long for clear, sweet, pure fresh air... *(struggles with his emotions)*.

The Huns chuck everything they can at us, and we just have to grin and bear it, and breathe in the stench... and I try not to look at the mutilated bodies of the horses everywhere.

Lights fade and rise again.

SCENE 6

A front-line trench. There is an explosion, then things quieten down.

The men are resting in their trench. They sing to the tune of 'What a friend we have in Jesus' but sing a different version.

MEN   When this blasted war is over,

O' how happy I shall be,

When I get my civvy clothes on, no more soldiering for me.

No more standing to in trenches,

Only one more church parade,

No more shivering on the fire-step,

No more Ticklers marmalade.

Their song is broken off as Lieutenant Wentworth appears, blowing his whistle furiously.

WENTWORTH On the fire-step, lads! Up you get! Bayonets fixed. Steady yourselves... Fire! Keep on firing. *(He blows his whistle, and all the men scramble over the rostra into no-man's land.)*

The following dialogue is all disembodied, heard as thoughts over the din of the action.

SOLDIER I'm firing blindly, our boys are machine-gunning them down, but they keep on coming, their bayonets glinting at the ready. I am truly terrified, and I want to run in the opposite direction, but I can't let my mates down. I am an automaton, loading, firing, loading, firing but still they keep on coming...

WENTWORTH That's it, lads, keep up the firing. There are gaps in their formation; the barbed wire has stopped them.

SOLDIER   No, Sir! Their bombardment has created a gap; it's blown a hole, and they've found it, Sir!

WENTWORTH Pick them off as they come through. That's it, lads... they have decided to retreat. Now it's our turn. *(He loudly blows his whistle.)* After them lads, move forward at a pace, we'll give them a taste of their own medicine.

SOLDIER   We are now pouring through the gap in the barbed wire, picking them off as they run... we are trampling, stumbling, over the dead Huns. We have to run over the dead and the dying, but now we have left our trench and picked up speed there is a feeling of exhilaration, of doing our duty, that's why we are here... but then it starts up... the Huns are shelling us and we begin to fall, right, left and centre. *(The sound of heavy shelling).* Mown down like animals having achieved... nothing... a pointless waste of men and the Lieutenant orders us back to our trench. Out in Dead Man's land there are more unburied soldiers, hundreds of our lads laying alongside the Huns... what a terrible waste.

WENTWORTH Well done, lads! I'm proud of you... now you've had seven days at the front line you can have your seven days back at the billets. You can even go to a show and see the entertainers, the good old optimists...

Lights fade and come up again.

SCENE 7

*A makeshift acting area back at the billets. The men
line up along the front of the stage with their backs
to the audience. Their focus is centre stage where an
entertainer appears; they applaud enthusiastically.*

ENTERTAINER Thank you lads for your warm
welcome. I've come with some advice from
our Generals, who are always thinking of
you and your welfare...

*There is general laughter with someone shouting out
"Who are you kidding?" And "Get on with it mate!"*

ENTERTAINER Don't Worry: when you are a soldier you
can be in one of two places: A dangerous
place or a safe place.

If you're in a safe place... don't worry.

If you're in a dangerous place you can be
one of two things: one is wounded and the
other is not.

If you're wounded, it is dangerous or slight.
If it's slight... don't worry.

If it's dangerous then one of two things will
happen:

You'll die or you'll recover. If you recover...
don't worry. If you die... you can't worry.

In these circumstances a soldier never
worries.

And so, lads, let's sing the words we all
love *(Sung to the tune of Auld Land Syne)*
they sum it all up!

"We're here because we're here because
We're here because we're here.

We're here because we're here because
We're here because we're here."

The men repeat the song as they leave the stage.

Lights gradually dim and rise on a trench.

SCENE 8

*In this reserve trench where the men can find some rest,
two of them are looking upwards and concentrating on a
dogfight in the sky.*

GEORGE *(Looking up into the sky)* Can you see them?
The sun is shining in my face.

ERNIE *(Shielding his eyes)* Yes! They seem to be flying
over Cambrai. There's going to be a fight...
there's (Scanning the sky) four of our chaps
and...one, two, three German planes. My
God, they're going at it hammer and tongs.

GEORGE   Do you think it's exciting being a pilot?

ERNIE   Well... *(Laughing)* there's no mud and no
rats up there!

GEORGE   I could have been an ace pilot if I hadn't
been born poor.

ERNIE   A lethal Icarus flying through the skies with
a machine gun.

GEORGE   I can tell you're a grammar schoolboy
(Teasing him) You use words I've never
heard of mate!

ERNIE   Those Hun pilots wanted to attack our
forward trench...

GEORGE *(Jumping up)* They've got one!

ERNIE   Poor bastard!

GEORGE   Whose side are you on?

ERNIE   Ours of course! But he's still a poor dead Hun bastard...

GEORGE *(Exhilarated)* Look! Look! *(Pointing upwards)* There goes another one... it's burst into flames... there's only one left.

Light fades and rises on Lieutenant Wentworth and the Sergeant.

SCENE 9

The Sergeant-Major's dug out.

He crouches over a large mailbag filled with letters and parcels. A lamp lights up his face and helps him read the names of the men as they line up to get their mail. This is acted as a tableau while Wentworth explains what happens when they are delivered. The Sergeant-Major in the background is calling out names ...

We hear Perkins, Evans, Harris, or any surnames which apply to the actors. Some men open up their parcels as they move away; others read their letters.

WENTWORTH   The mail has just come in. It was brought up on the ammunition limbers. I heard the cry "Mail Up" and then the running feet of the men. The mail is brought up at night, but the men have to unload the ammunition before they get their mail. You should see them working at speed along a chain and passing the shells swiftly to the

> gunpits, but we officers have to sit still and wait for our letter to be brought to us by our servants. It's a sore trial to our patience, part of the price we pay for our rank.

The tableau ends with the Sergeant-Major shaking his head to some of the men. Finally, the bag is empty. He turns it upside down and gives it a good shake, and shrugs. The men who have letters go off to read them. Those that don't go off disgruntled. The Sergeant-Major walks off with his bag and the lamp.

The light grows dimmer.

WENTWORTH It's odd to think how far these letters travel and how safely they arrive despite being brought up under shellfire. Letters from their mothers, their wives, their sweethearts. They sit around their fires in silence, reading by the light of the jumping flames. War seems to have ceased for a little, while the men's memories will be back in 'Blighty', affections stirring... and when I look up *(looks up at the sky),* such a night with the stars like a pattern set in ebony...quite beautiful...

OFFICER'S SERVANT *(Saluting, then handing Wentworth a bundle of letters)* There are several for you, Sir *(hands them over).* And this bundle is for the other Officers, will you take them and distribute them, Sir?

WENTWORTH Yes! *(He takes them)* I'll hand them out, thank you.

The servant salutes, then leaves Wentworth on his own.

WENTWORTH Such precious things, these letters. I watch the Captain's face as he reads his.

Sometimes it seems they do not tell him what he wants to hear. *(He shrugs)* Oh well, back to the hole in the ground we call our mess, such a grand name for a muddy hole... we have tables, but the men don't. A table becomes a luxury here...

Lights fade and then come up again on the newsboy.

NEWSBOY *(Waving a paper)* Germany halted on the River Marne. The Allies have gained the upper hand. Paris is saved again.

Lights dim and come up again.

SCENE 10

A front line trench where the men are getting ready to go over the top.

One of them, Jack is obviously in a state of nervous collapse and shakes a great deal. A loud whistle is heard further down the trench. Jack scrambles over with the others, but then comes back into the trench obviously shell-shocked and trembling. He is crying and shaking when the sergeant appears in a furious temper.

SERGEANT What the hell do you think you are doing? Get up and go like the rest!

JACK No! I can't...I can't do it no more...

SERGEANT *(Pulling him up)* You bloody well can! *(Trying to get him on the firestep)* Get up, I tell you...get up and start firing.

Jack struggles with the sergeant who is trying to get him up and over.

JACK *(Breaking free and cowering down in the trench)* It's no good, I can't face it anymore...not anymore. *(He puts his hands over his ears.)* It's the noise, the stink, the barrage on and on...

SERGEANT *(Standing over him)* Private Webster, I am telling you, ordering you to get up and go.

JACK No! I won't, not anymore *(He starts to cry bitterly.)* Not anymore...I'm finished, like Billy was

SERGEANT You're finished all right, you bloody coward! This means the firing squad... I'll give you one more order, "Get up and over!"

JACK I'm not doing it, not anymore.

The Sergeant pulls him up.

The sound of machine guns gets louder, and the lights dim and rise on the Narrator.

NARRATOR So many young men shot for desertion or cowardice. By the end of this terrible war, 346 British soldiers will be shot – this equals approximately one poor shell-shocked soldier shot every five days. That's nothing the British Army can be proud of... not when we compare this figure with the 48 soldiers the Germans shot. And the French, well their military courts randomly select soldiers to be shot as an example of what will happen to cowards... this tactic is even more shocking when we think that the French shot about 600 of their soldiers. Court Marshalls were brief with the accused under-represented. We British shot two poor exhausted men for sleeping at their posts. *(He shakes his head.)*

Yes! Facing the firing squad for being too tired to stay awake after night after night of cannonades and rockets... and we may call the Germans Huns, Bosch, Monsters but with troops who have outnumbered we Brits by two to one, the number is 48... only 48... just think about that...we will shoot nearly 300 more...

The lights fade on the Narrator and come up again.

SCENE 11

A support trench.

Some men are trying to sleep; others read their letters or books.

BERT *(Looking upwards as he crouches in the trench)* There goes another flare. The Huns are busy tonight.

RON   The way they light up the night sky, it's like carnival time.

BERT   It's to see we don't creep up on them.

RON   Creep! I'm not leaving this trench tonight, mate.

BERT   You will, mate, if Lieutenant Wentworth says,"Get up and go!" or if that bloody Sergeant blasts our eardrums.

RON   I might not, I might just stay put...

BERT   You'd be shot Ron, for disobeying orders, like Jack. He got up, went over, ran a few yards, and then turned and jumped back into our trench. He'd been in a state since Billy drowned, mind.

RON   Yeah, I know! Desertion in the line of duty, poor sod.

BERT   But for days he hadn't stopped shaking. He had become a nervous wreck. His nerves were shattered.

RON   I know, I know! They shot him with two others from the battalion down the line.

BERT   Mates shooting mates! It's not like shooting the Huns, is it? Would you shoot me Ron?

RON   An order's an order, isn't it? If I don't shoot, I get shot. It's the rules of war...blasted rules are rules.

BERT   I wish this bloody rain would stop. *(He looks up to the sky)*. The only good thing about it is the flares have stopped... perhaps I can doze off.

RON   Yeah! Have forty winks and think of home.

BERT   I'm going round the corner where there's some shelter. *(He moves away from Ron and covers himself in his blankets.)*

Silence, then flashes of light. Some of the men, who have been reading their letters or books, stop and start to sing together.

MEN   Hush, here comes a whizz-bang.

Hush, here comes a whizz-bang.

Now you soldier men get down those stairs,

Down in your dugouts and say your prayers.

Hush, here comes a whizz-bang.

And it's making right for you.

And you'll see all the wonders on no-man's land,

If a whizz-bang hits you.

The lights fade and rise on the men now singing another song.

MEN   Gassed last night, and gassed the night before.

Going to get gassed tonight if we never

Get gassed anymore When we're gassed, we're sick as we can be

For Phosgene and mustard gas is much too Much for me.

The light fades and rises on Lucy sitting in a garden in Canterbury.

SCENE 12

LUCY *(Closing her book with a snap)* I thought coming home on leave from the front would bring me some peace of mind *(shaking her head)*, but it hasn't. At night all I can think of is the medical centre, and I wonder how they can manage with one less pair of hands with the wounded being brought in. Truckload-after-truckload. Poor Vera! She will be dreadfully overworked. The time of the mustard gas attacks was horror personified and I can never ever get it out of my mind... yesterday, at Mama's tea-party for the Sewing Guild which she really held to show me off to the women because I'm doing 'my bit' for the war... this poor woman joined me here in the garden...

Lucy moves to a garden chair where she sits next to Mrs Parker.

MRS PARKER *(Holding up a piece of paper which she shows to Lucy)* As you are going back to France soon, I thought I might ask you to help us, Lucy. My husband and I are desperate to find out where our son is buried. *(She wipes her eyes with her handkerchief.)* We need to find his body, so we can bring him home. He is, was, our only child *(She starts to cry)...* If only we knew where he is... I've written all you might need on this card... *(She reads)* Private Charles Parker of the Hampshire Fusiliers... he is – was – only eighteen... a kind boy... just a boy, really. *(She tries to control herself)*. It was after the last great battle we received a telegram which told us he was missing, presumed killed... but that word 'presumed' gives us hope... but then the hope vanishes... hope doesn't comfort us for very long... can you understand?

LUCY *(Taking the woman's hand)* Yes, I can, Mrs Parker. Hope is difficult to cling on to...

MRS PARKER We gave Charles my maiden name, Carrington, so his full name is Charles Carrington Parker. There cannot be another young man with the same name, can there? We have written to the Red Cross's Wounded and Missing Enquiry Department in London, but they haven't been able to help us. He would have been wearing his army tag with his number in it... that tag would identify him, *(tearfully)* wouldn't it?

LUCY   Yes, we see they still have their tag around their necks at the Casualty Clearing Stations.

MRS PARKER   As you work so closely with the Red Cross, Lucy, you could try to find out. You might find someone from his regiment who would know where his body is buried. You see, we realise now that he has been killed, he's dead... we no longer get letters from him... he wrote such caring, beautiful letters to us. *(She breaks down)* No more letters *(shaking her head)*. If he were alive, wounded, he would send us a letter... a letter is a very precious thing...

LUCY *(Comforting her)* I will do what I can, Mrs Parker *(taking the card from her)*. I will ask men who might know. I will do my best... I promise...

Lights fade on them.

Lucy moves back to the garden bench.

LUCY *(Picking up her book but not opening it)* How can we tell the truth, the horror of it all, when the Army censors see to it that the truth's never revealed in our letters? We are all compliant in maintaining the fiction that we are all doing fine, just fine! How ridiculous! Poor Mrs Parker, she has no idea... missing is just a euphemism for "blown to bits!" Head, arms, legs all scattered over a muddy landscape, trodden on by other soldiers... ground into the earth by horses hooves... feet, hooves, artillery wheels, wagon wheels... it is not like Waterloo where relatives could wander over the battlefield looking for the body of a loved one... this is not 1815, and we have the power to blow men to bits... I could not tell Mrs Parker the truth... there will be no body to find... poor eighteen-year-old Charles Carrington Parker was probably blown to smithereens.

Lucy's Mama appears.

MAMA   Lucy! Do come in, the light now is not good enough for reading; it's too dim... come inside...

LUCY   I was thinking about poor, Mrs Parker, the woman who joined me in the garden yesterday.

MAMA   I really didn't want her to bother you. She came out here before I had noticed she had left the sitting room.

LUCY   It wasn't bothersome...

MAMA   She does go on about finding her son's body. I am sure they will find a grave somewhere when this is over... she needs patience I think... and with the Americans in the fight, it should surely be coming to an end...

Lights dim and then come up again.

SCENE 13

A corner of a support trench.

Some men are looking for lice in their coats. Others are reading. One man is writing in his journal.

RON   Hey Taffy! How's it going with you?

TAFFY *(Stamping and shifting his feet around)* If I don't stamp around, this mud seems to really suck me down. Turns to muddy cement it does. Really nasty stuff, but I try and be cheerful like the other chaps.

RON In the last four years, I've been in trenches with mud up to my armpits, and there's nothing to be cheerful about with mud up to your chin.

TAFFY That's an exaggeration, isn't it?

RON Okay, up to my waist! Will that satisfy your 'delicate sense of gaining information?'

TAFFY There's no need to get shirty with me, Ron. A fact is a fact.

RON Well, as I was stuck in a trench for over a week with nothing happening, it felt like the mud was rising up and overwhelming me, smothering me even. I've had four years of mud hell with short trips to 'Blighty' that don't last long enough. I'm an authority on mud, right!

TAFFY You'll be telling me next that the rats are getting even bigger than cats. *(He gestures with his arms)* "As big as this Taffy! The biggest rats you've ever seen!"

RON *(Angrily)* Well, they were, I can tell you! Well-fed on our boys' corpses... I hate rats, they get big on dead horses, too.

TAFFY Don't talk about it – it gives me the horrors, the shivers. I just want to think about my Ma's warm kitchen in Llandysul and the smell of her Welsh cakes... lovely!

RON And I want to be home in Preston with no bloody duck boards and no blasted mud, and best of all, no bastard Hun tossing in hand-grenades.

All the men come together and sing.

MEN I want to go home; I want to go home. I don't want to go in the trenches no more, where whizz-bangs and shrapnel whistle and roar.

Take me over the sea, where the Germans can't get at me.

Oh my, I don't want to die, I want to go home.

The light fades and comes up on the Narrator.

NARRATOR We are finally going to turn the tables and strike back with force. We are going to smash the Hindenburg line to smithereens. The Germans won't know what's hit them...

Lights fade and come up on the newsboy who crosses the stage.

NEWSBOY *(Waving paper)* Read all about it... Hindenburg line is smashed. The Germans are retreating all along the Western Front. The Huns are on the run.

Lights fade and come up again.

SCENE 14

A front line trench with only two soldiers in it. Standing at ease while smoking cigarettes.

RON   Hey! Have you still got your old Princess Royal tin? *(He gets a small tin out of his pocket.)* Mine's full of fags.

TAFFY   Yeah! Isn't it nice to know the Princess Mary was thinking about us?

RON *(Miming Taffy)* "Isn't it nice to know the Princess Mary was thinking about us!" Look mate, the Princess couldn't have cared less. It's all political manipulation, isn't it? Keep the troops happy, con them into thinking the Royal Family is thinking about them, stuck in the trenches. "We, the Royals are with each and every one of you brave boys." We've been conned for four years...

TAFFY   I liked what I got in my tin. Now I keep my fags nice and dry in it. I liked getting my tin.

RON   Cannon fodder! That's what we are. Come the revolution, and they'll all be swept-away. Gone! Just like the Tsar of Russia...

TAFFY   That's a bit harsh, isn't it?

RON   Look mate, the British Royals are all Germans, and here we are still facing Germans. Behind that barbed wire are all their German cousins, trying to kill us... bloody Huns... bloody Bosch!

They listen to a distant barrage, then machine gunfire for a minute or two as they smoke.

TAFFY   Wilf down the line had a lucky escape. He showed me his pocket bible what he keeps in his breast pocket. We were queued up for the latrines...

RON *(Contemptuously)* Ugh! A bible carrier... a bible basher too! I hate them.

TAFFY   It has a big hole in the middle. It stopped a bullet. Wilf says it was God directing his Guardian Angel to keep him safe. It touched his skin but stopped in his bible.

RON *(Laughing)* It wasn't God. It wasn't his Guardian Angel – it was just bloody luck! Get it Taffy? Good luck!

TAFFY   Don't you believe in God, Ron?

RON   I'm an atheist. I'm not here because of King and Country, or God. I'm here because I got bloody conscripted. Got it? And I've been here for too bloody long.

TAFFY   Well, I pray all the time that God will keep me safe. My Ma would die of a broken heart if I didn't get back.

RON   Boyo, I'm not praying. I'm getting out of this war; it's gone on for too long... who the hell knows when it will end? I'm going back to 'Blighty' before any blasted German kills me.

TAFFY   But you're not due for any leave, and you haven't been wounded.

RON   No! But I'm master of my own destiny boyo.

TAFFY   What do you mean?

RON   All I have to do is make sure I get wounded.

TAFFY   You could get killed, not wounded and if they think it's a 'Blighty' wound, they'll shoot you for cowardice.

RON   Look mate, I've a plan, see. If I light a fag and put my right hand just over the top of the trench, some Bosch sniper is going to aim and get me.

TAFFY   But you couldn't work after the war Ron, you'll be a cripple. Maimed for life.

RON   I'd be alive, Taffy. Alive! Next time our officers send us over the top I could be dead. *(He opens his tin.)* The only things not damp in this muddy piss-hole are my fags. *(He gets one out and starts to light it.)*

TAFFY   Don't do it, Ron, not your right hand.

RON *(Laughing)* Taffy boyo, I'm what's called ambidextrous. I can use my left hand just as well as my right hand. Anyway, it's got to be my right hand as it will look suspicious if it's my left, and they will have to declare me unfit for military service.

TAFFY *(Looks at Ron in disbelief)* But you've told me. I could report you to the Sergeant.

RON *(Smiling and shaking his head)* But you won't, will you, Taffy? Because you're my best mate, and you wouldn't like to have me shot like they did to Jack.

TAFFY *(He draws on his cigarette slowly)* Yeh, you're right. I couldn't do it to you.

Ron lights a cigarette and then places his right hand on top of the parapet. There are flashes of light and machine gunfire, then silence.

RON   Come on you bloody, Hun... are you bloody sleeping?

Silence. Then a single shot.

RON *(He doubles up in pain)* Oh! The bastard has got me! Bloody hell! *(He writhes in pain.)* I've lost some fingers! *(He shouts at Taffy)* Get the bloody orderlies... I'm wounded. *(He falls to his knees).* It's 'Blighty' for me... 'Blighty', here I come... wounded but alive *(He cries with pain and relief.)* Yes! I've made it...

Taffy runs off to get the orderlies. We begin to hear a melancholy tune on a mouth organ. There is no barrage.

Lights fade and come up on the Narrator.

NARRATOR   The guns did fall silent on the eleventh day of the eleventh month at the eleventh hour...but there was no jubilance in the trenches. Men were too traumatised; there were so many dead. Friendships that went through thick and thin only to be blasted out by war... too many mates sucked into the depths of muddy craters or left mutilated on barbed wire. Too much horror for the mind to carry.

Lights fade and come up on the Newsboy who crosses the stage.

NEWSBOY *(Waving a newspaper)* The German Kaiser abdicates and flees the country. An armistice is signed... the fighting is over. Read all about it. We've won the war!

Lights fade and come up again on Lucy.

SCENE 15

Outside the Red Cross Centre.

LUCY   Just silence, unbelievable, unreal silence after four years of continuous shelling. A world of gangrene, amputations, sepsis, fractured limbs, and now an extended silence...with time to think about all those beautiful young men buried in mud. Thousands of them... missing... when the numbers are all added up, it will astonish us... yes! When I get home, the war will still confront me with its horrors... there will be amputees, young men on crutches, the maimed survivors who must somehow make a life for themselves. The world is not going to be the same for me ever again... there has been a great slaughter of my generation.

Lucy starts to cry.

Vera enters, carrying a small suitcase.

VERA *(Going to comfort Lucy)* I want to cry too, Lucy, but I'm trying to be brave... it is all over, at last.

LUCY   I've been brave for too long, just carrying on, and on... and what upsets me the most is the stupid people I have to go back to in Canterbury.

VERA   Stupid?

LUCY   Yes! Whenever I would have home leave and be told by my relatives *(She mimes an aunt)* "Oh! How uplifting it must be Lucy, to actually be on active service in a hospital at the Front. Truly inspiring!" Oh! How little they knew of the horrors we have seen, sitting in their comfortable Canterbury drawing rooms, safe and sound and deluded.

VERA   We shall return very different girls to the ones we were in August 1914. The war has ended, but there is no jubilation here...

LUCY   No! Just silent troops and a dull ache for the dead.

VERA   I know my remembrance will grow dim as the years go by, and that may be for the best.

LUCY   The war is over, and a new age is beginning for all of us... but the dead are dead, and will never ever return to those who loved them... that is the final and only truth.

The lights dim. We hear a bugle play "The Reveille" and then "The Last Post".

The lights fade on Lucy and Vera. When it is dim, one by one, the characters join them on stage, silently like ghosts, with torches held under their chins to make them ghost-like. They hold poppy wreaths in the other hand as "The Last Post" is repeated.

Poppies are scattered all over the stage area.

Lights fade down.

The End.

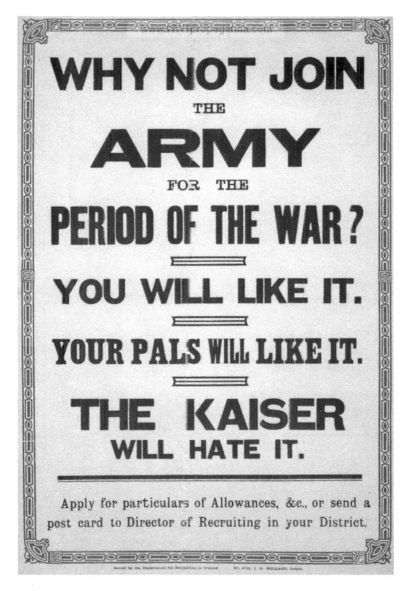

Propaganda Poster 1914. Image courtesy Oxford University

Propaganda poster 1914. Image courtesy IWM.

Nursing sisters and orderlies at Malmesbury Hospital, 1918.
Photo: www.wiltshireatwar.org

Above: British Vickers machine gun crew wearing PH-type anti-gas helmets. Near Ovillers during the Battle of the Somme, July 1916. *Below:* British soldiers with Mark V tanks advancing at battle of the St. Quentin canal, 1918.

Above: British soldiers from the Border Regiment resting in dugouts, at the Battle of the Somme, 1916.

Above: US Marines in a trench. c.1918 *Opposite:* German soldiers *(top)* and advancing *(below).* Photo: G. Bauer/pexels

More plays to perform:

Noor by Azma Dar
ISBN 978-1-912430-72-7 £9.99
Humane by Polly Creed
ISBN 978-1-912430-57-4 £9.99
Wollstonecraft Live! by Kaethe Fine
ISBN 978-1-912430-61-1 £11.99
Diary of a Hounslow Girl by Ambreen Razia
ISBN 978-0-9536757-9-1 £8.99
Harvest by Manjula Padmanabhan
ISBN 978-0-9536757-7-7 £9.99
Mistaken: Annie Besant in India by Rukhsana
Ahmad ISBN 978-0-9551566-9-4 £7.99
Penetration by Carolyn Lloyd-Davies
ISBN 978-1-912430-63-5 £9.99
The Curious Lives of Shakespeare and Cervantes by Asa
Palomera ISBN 978-1-911501-13-8 £9.99
The Marvellous Adventures of Mary Seacole by Cleo
Sylvestre ISBN 978-1-912430-59-8 £8.99
Three Mothers by Matilda Velevitch
ISBN 978-1-912430-35-2 £9.99

For collections of plays see:

www.aurorametro.com